Seeing Sugar

Seeing Sugar

by

Cynthia L. Brinson

SCHOLASTIC INC.
New York Toronto London Auckland Sydney
Mexico City New Delhi Hong Kong Buenos Aires

ISBN 0-439-71695-0

12 11 10 9 8 7 6 5 4 3   5 6 7 8 9/0

Printed in the U.S.A.   40

First Scholastic printing, November 2004

Set in Stempel Scheidler
Book design by Teresa Kietlinski

For three
amazing
guys.
—C.L.B.

Contents

On Monday, Kate Loved School

·1·

KATE twisted up the tire swing and climbed on in two seconds flat. Spinning, spinning, spinning, she leaned back and looked into the crown of her old maple tree. On Monday, this swirling world of green had reminded her of the new soccer field at Maplewood School. But on Tuesday, she saw the cafeteria's murky split-pea soup. Spinning, spinning, spinning, she shouted, "I *hate* Maplewood School!"

Why did everything have to change? Until now, fourth grade had been fun. It felt good to be in school, like she was part of a play that couldn't go on without her. And Miss Burke was Kate's favorite teacher ever! She was friendly and tall and had red hair that danced on her shoulders and swung against her chin. Her skirts were just like Scottish kilts, plaid with giant safety pins. Kate thought her teacher would look great playing bagpipes in a parade.

"Miss Burke sounds wonderful," Kate's mother had said one afternoon as they sat on the front steps with a bowl of sugared popcorn.

"She wears knee-highs that match her sweaters," Kate said. "And penny loafers with actual pennies. Shiny ones, like she saved them up just for the first day of school." That was one reason she was Kate's all-time favorite; Miss Burke was as excited as Kate was on the first day of school. She knew all about the good jitters that came with each new year. It was nothing like the way Kate's brother felt. Andy would trade school any day for a broken-in baseball glove and a stinging metal bat.

Not even Jenny or Lauren shared Kate's enthusiasm, and they were her best friends. "I'd be happy if vacation lasted fifty-two weeks a year," Jenny would say. She was a natural fish-monkey, swimming in the lake and climbing in the woods all summer long.

Lauren had sewn a patch on her backpack that said I'D RATHER BE SHOPPING.

Kate liked summer vacation too; who wouldn't? But then she couldn't wait for school to start again. This year, on the first day of school, she got up early, put on the jeans and T-shirt she had picked out the night before, and ate a bagel, all before Andy had opened one eye. Kate liked walking the two blocks to school under spreading maples as old as her own tree. She liked listening to the songbirds and watching twitchy brown squirrels race across the lawns.

Kate was the first student to enter 4-B. Miss Burke met her with a smile on her coral lips, and a sparkle in her green eyes. "You look like a girl who would appreciate a seat up front," she had said, and tapped the desk nearest her own.

The desk was front and center. Kate could pass out papers and listen to Miss Burke talk on the phone. She would hear her warn the principal that Sammy Sullivan was on his way to the office. Kate slid into her seat and waited for the buses to arrive, waited for Jenny and

Lauren. It was the first time since pre-school that the three of them were in the same class. Kate's whole neighborhood had heard their screams the day that room assignments came in the mail. "Fourth grade is going to be great!" they kept saying.

And it had been great. Kate handed out papers and eavesdropped on every telephone call. She even fell in love with geography, thanks to the neon globe on Miss Burke's desk. If a student was from another part of the country, or another country altogether, Miss Burke turned to the globe. When a lesson mentioned a city or a continent, the globe was passed around the room. Kate had never been interested in geography before, but by the middle of September she was an expert at pointing out places in hot pink, zinnia orange, and lizard green.

Of course, school still had its draw-backs. The cafeteria still served its carpet glue soups and petrified fruit slices. The bathrooms still reeked, and the gym floor was so dirty you could take three showers on P.E. days and never feel clean.

But those things were normal for schools; they were to be expected. Sammy Sullivan was not. This boy lived to wipe Kate's smile right off her face. Sammy Sullivan was famous for his put-downs, sharp words that jabbed like needles. Miss Burke had put him in the first row, halfway back. Kate steered clear of him.

But not even the horrible Sammy Sullivan could put a damper on Miss Burke. She claimed that her mission in life was to make learning fun, even if it made her look a little crazy sometimes. Once she acted out a math problem that twisted her into a pretzel, and Sammy's sharp claps silenced the room. "Your comedy routine won't win any awards," he blurted out.

But Miss Burke only glared at him, a long, cool look that stopped him short. Kate loved school!

Until Tuesday, that is. The day everything changed. The day someone new showed up in class and inspired Kate to spin on her tire swing shouting, "I *hate* Maplewood School!"

On Tuesday,
Everything
Changed

·2·

TUESDAY started out with blue skies and chalky white clouds. On the way to school Kate spotted a flock of bright yellow goldfinches and seven squirrels with cheeks inflated like balloons. She knew all those nuts meant that soon a winter wind would sweep the clouds into angry streaks. Just thinking about those bone-freezing days made her shiver.

Most of the class was already seated when Kate hung up her backpack and headed for her desk. She stopped to spin the globe before sitting down, just like she did every day. Then, even before it came to a stop, Miss Burke picked up the globe and held it above her head.

"We'll skip the Daily Edit today because we have a new place to find on the globe." The excitement in her voice said something was up. Miss Burke opened the classroom door. "Come in, come in," she said into the hallway. Then she turned to her students. "And we have a new class-mate to help us."

A small girl walked into the room. Her caramel hair hung all the way to her waist, and she wore a lavender backpack that seemed to weigh more than she did. Miss Burke rested one hand on the girl's shoul-der and held the globe up high with her other hand. She looked like the Statue of Liberty of American Schools.

Miss Burke's grin spread across her whole face. *Delighted* was the word that popped into Kate's head. "I want you all to welcome Miss Sugar Rose Simms to our class."

"Welcome, Sugar Rose," chanted some of the students.

Miss Burke took Sugar's backpack and gave her the globe in one swift movement. She hurried over to hang up the pack and then hurried back, while the new girl stared at the dull brown floor tiles. "Sugar Rose is from Georgia," Miss Burke said. "Can you find that state for us, Sugar Rose?"

The new girl spun the globe against the pink flowers in her dress. "Here it is, ma'am," she said in a voice that sounded like a bird's peep.

"Hold it up so we can all see," Miss Burke said.

So Sugar Rose Simms held up the neon globe and pointed to a lizard green spot with the polished pink pointer finger of her right hand. Georgia was situated just above Florida, as everyone knew it would be.

Then something horrible happened. While the new girl stood there watching, Miss Burke leaned over and whispered to Kate, "It would be so nice to give this desk to our new friend; I know you won't mind taking the empty seat behind Jenny."

Kate was shocked right out of her chair. She scooped up books and papers and her bright red pencil box, as Miss Burke motioned to the new girl. Sugar Rose glanced at Kate for one quick second before sliding into the desk. Now *she* was front and center.

Kate carried her things to the empty seat at the back of the room. She felt her face grow as red as the pencil box and looked down at those old floor tiles. She didn't know if she was mad as fire or about to cry.

During math, spelling, and current events Kate sat as still as stone. No words made it to or from her brain. Not through her ears. Not through her eyes. Not flowing out of her pencil. Kate didn't hear the equations that her classmates called out. She didn't hear the vocabulary words Miss Burke recited. She didn't even hear the opinions batted back and forth about what had caused the flooding in the Midwest.

What Kate noticed was color: the kelly green of Jenny's baseball cap, the turquoise of Lauren's new barrettes, Mike's jet-black hair, and the red highlights in a single strand of her own chin-length hair.

And Kate noticed odors, everyday school smells that suddenly seemed huge and ugly. Rachel's leftover cheese sandwich made her nose itch. Christopher's hair gel gave her a headache. And Tom's sneakers made her want to throw up.

Kate felt so bad inside that she couldn't think or hear straight. That's why she didn't stand up when the teacher announced lunchtime. That's why she just sat there the first and second times Jenny said, "Let's go eat." That's why she didn't answer when the cafeteria lady asked, "What would you like?"

And things only got worse after lunch. Kate took her seat at the back of the room and felt like she was in another state. If Georgia was way up there at the front, then she must be in Alaska.

When everyone was seated again after recess, Miss Burke asked Sugar Rose to tell

the class about herself. "Yes ma'am," said
Sugar. She stood next to Kate's old desk
and faced the class.

"Her hair is as long as my old Barbie's,"
Lauren whispered.

"And her nose is tiny like Barbie's too,"
Jenny whispered back.

Sammy Sullivan leaned into the aisle
and sneered. "Maybe she's the new
Georgia Peach Pit Barbie."

Miss Burke glared at Sammy, and Kate
stared at Sugar to see what her friends
were talking about. But she was too far
away to see Sugar clearly. She got out a
book to read instead. And even though
Kate didn't listen to a single word Sugar
said, she could tell that her voice was sick-
eningly sweet.

That was the Tuesday afternoon Kate
twirled on her tire swing hating
Maplewood School. She kept remember-

ing how the new girl with her long silky hair had waltzed into the classroom and stolen her seat. She could hear the girl calling Miss Burke *ma'am* in her too-sweet voice, and suddenly a lump the size of a peach pit was rising in her throat. Spinning, spinning, spinning, Kate shouted, "I *hate* Sugar!"

Dinner
at the
Martins'

·3·

KATE'S mother cut three oranges into thin round suns. She was making her annual Fall Is Here dinner, deep bowls of chili with hot crusty bread, and oranges juicy with vitamin C. This Martin family ritual marked the official end of summer and the beginning of cool weather. Usually the meal made Kate feel cozy and part of the season, but not this year.

"Wow, it's getting cold out there," Andy said, sliding into his chair at the kitchen table as if he were sliding into home base.

Just home from work, their father left his laptop next to the laundry room door and came to the table. "It's supposed to get down to forty degrees tonight. So long, warm, humid weather. Hello, crisp fall air!"

Their mother finished ladling the chili and sat down. "Thank you for the food we eat," she began, and the family joined in. "Thank you for the world so sweet. Thank you for the birds that sing. Thank you, God, for everything."

It was almost October. Kate pictured pumpkins on the front porch, frost on the lawn, and—of course—school. Once wonderful, now terrible, *school*!

"Hey, where were you today?" Andy said. "I looked in your classroom and someone else was in your place."

Kate only glared at him, a long cool look she hoped would shut him up.

The look worked on Andy but not on their mother. "Oh? Has Miss Burke rearranged your seats already?" She smiled, practically winking at Kate. "There are always certain personalities that just don't work together."

Kate's father actually did wink. "What did Sammy Sullivan say now?"

Kate let a hunk of bread sink to the bottom of her chili. "It wasn't him," she said. "We got a new girl, and she has my seat now." Kate stabbed at the soggy bread with her butter knife. She let her hair fall into her face.

Her mother picked up Kate's soup

spoon and handed it to her. "I see."

"Wait a minute." Andy jumped in. "Are you saying you got tossed out of your precious teacher's-pet seat?"

Kate glared at him.

Kate's father patted her hand, exactly as if he thought she was four years old. "I'm sure the teacher only meant to make the new girl as comfortable as possible."

Kate pulled her hand away and went back to poking around in her chili. The bread had already disintegrated.

Their mother turned to Andy. "Tell us about baseball practice today." Even though Kate didn't want to talk about what happened at school, she wished they didn't have to talk about baseball. Again. Still. Always!

"We've got next year's play-offs locked up." Andy's team was called the Slammers, and they always had the play-offs locked up. They won the pennant every year.

"You're pretty sure of yourself," their father said.

Andy grinned. "You bet I am! You should see this new player we've got, a kid named Chet, from Georgia. Best batter I've ever seen in my life."

"You're pretty terrific at batting too."

"Not like this guy," Andy said. "We're supremely lucky his family landed in Maplewood." He peered at Kate over his water glass. "Hey, Chet has a younger sister named Sugar Rose, of all things. Is that the girl who nabbed your seat?"

Their father cleared his throat, signaling that the conversation was over. "This is a wonderful Fall Is Here meal," he said.

Their mother slid the plate of cinnamon-and-sugar-sprinkled orange slices toward

Kate. Then she moved the sugar bowl closer too. "Just in case you want them sweeter."

Kate pushed her chair away from the table. "Sugar makes me sick."

Day
and Night
Dreaming

.4.

FROM her bedroom on the second floor, Kate looked down at the maple tree in the yard. There was a bird on her tire swing, taking in the last rays of sunshine. Everything looked different from this point of view. Kate saw that the tree, which seemed so green this afternoon, was already orange at the tips of its branches. She wondered if the bird would fly south for the winter.

That night in her dreams, Kate rode her tire swing as the familiar old maple spun into Miss Burke's neon globe. She saw children playing beneath tropical palm trees and snow-covered evergreens. She heard the cries of seagulls and screech owls. She smelled sweet coconut milk and pungent pinecones. The kinds of trees and birds that Kate saw in the children's backyards depended upon where she was on the earth.

Wednesday
Was
Worse

·5·

ON Wednesday morning, Sammy Sullivan slithered past Kate's desk and hissed, "Devastating demotion, huh?"

Kate forced herself not to flinch. Ignoring the snake completely, she took out paper and pencil and searched the blackboard for the Daily Edit. Miss Burke always wrote a sentence about one of the kids in her class, like *Kate Martin loves geografy so much that she makes the world go around every day* (Then the class would change the *f* in *geografy* to *ph* and add a period.) Or, *Lauren, go directly to the mall do not pass Go do not collect two hundred dollars.* (And the class would supply periods after *mall* and *Go*, and capitalize the *d*s on *do*.)

But today the words were hard to read. Kate stretched as far forward in her seat as possible, so close to Jenny that she could smell her woodsy shampoo. "I can't even see the board," she whispered. "How can you stand sitting back here?"

Jenny laughed. "I don't *stand* sitting."

"Ha-ha."

Jenny turned around in her seat. "I'm glad you're back here with me."

"Thanks," Kate said. "I guess it's not so bad." Or it wouldn't be, if she could see the stupid blackboard.

"Who can tell me what changes we

need to make here?" Miss Burke said in her let's-get-down-to-business voice.

Usually Kate's hand flew up before anyone else's, but not today. And nobody else volunteered either. Kate kept her head down as Miss Burke's gaze traveled across the room. Finally, when the clock on the wall had ticked away at least thirty seconds, the teacher spoke. "Go ahead, Kate. I'm sure you can tell us what we need to do with this sentence."

Kate stood next to her cold, faraway Alaskan desk and peered at the blackboard. She was frozen. "Perhaps we need a capital letter, a change in tense, or a question mark," Miss Burke suggested.

Still Kate did not answer. She squinted like her father did when he stood at the kitchen window watching birds. "Looks like a chickadee," he'd say. Or, "I think that's a downy woodpecker." But even squeezing her eyes into teeny tiny slits, Kate could not read the words the teacher had written. She could feel Sammy Sullivan, the new girl, and the rest of the class waiting for her to speak.

Eventually, when it was clear that Kate couldn't complete the Daily Edit, Miss Burke asked Sugar Rose to help. "Yes, ma'am," Sugar said. "Toms turbo sneakers take him in and out up and around," she read. "We need an apostrophe mark before the *s* in *Toms*, and a comma between *out* and *up*." Simple as that, Miss Sugar Rose Simms came to the rescue while Kate's face burned.

In the cafeteria the lunch lady tapped her gigantic spoon against a pan of broccoli à la slime. "What would you like?"

Kate asked for chicken nuggets and a bowl of peaches that had only a few rotten spots. Then she took a carton of chocolate milk and sat at her usual table with Lauren and Jenny. Across the cafeteria, Miss Burke was leaning down to say something to Sugar Rose. Her red hair brushed against Sugar's caramel head. When Sugar motioned toward a table of sixth-graders Miss Burke put an arm around her shoulder and led her in that direction.

Sixth-graders were the oldest students at Maplewood School, and they always ate at the three tables closest to the playground doors. Kate had never seen a fourth-grader eat with them before, but there was Sugar, sitting between a boy wearing an Atlanta Braves jersey and Kate's own brother Andy.

"Look at that," Jenny said. "Sugar's at the sixth-grade table."

Lauren almost dropped her fork, but caught it in the knick of time. "Wow, she's lucky. Lucky *and* pretty."

Jenny picked up half of her cream cheese and jelly sandwich, squishing it until the soft center oozed out at the sides. "I liked Sugar's story about living in Georgia, especially the part about spending summers at the beach. I'd like to see her shell collection."

Kate dunked one of her chicken nuggets into a puddle of ketchup. "I'll bet that boy is her brother Chet. He's on Andy's baseball team."

"I think we should ask Sugar Rose to eat with us," Jenny said. "We sure could use another dodge ball player."

Kate saw Andy pointing at her, and Sugar looking her way. She didn't feel like getting to know the new girl.

"We promised Rachel we'd play four-square with her today. Let's ask Sugar Rose tomorrow," Lauren said.

I'll find a way to be absent, Kate thought.

***

Her mother was waiting on the front porch when Kate got home from school. "Sit down," she said, putting an arm around her daughter, just as Miss Burke had done with Sugar Rose. Kate was tired and glad to sit, glad to have her mother sitting next to her. They were quiet for a while, watching a black cat fling itself onto a roof across the street. A few feet away the neighbor's fat yellow cat slept on his back in the sunshine. Kate's mother gave her shoulder a little squeeze. "It's a jewel of a day, isn't it?"

"Yes, it's nice out." Kate wished that she could fall asleep in the grass or play away her troubles. She wished the new girl had never moved to town. She wished she still sat center stage, near Miss Burke and her globe. She wished everything were back to normal.

"How was school today?"

"Okay." Kate could tell that her mother knew she was upset, but she didn't want to talk about it. "We started a unit on Europe," she offered instead. "I got to find Portugal on the globe."

Kate's mother sighed. "I always liked geography and social studies. You'll love learning about the cultures of Europe."

The rowdy cat jumped down from the roof, raced across the street, leaped over the sidewalk, and pounced on the tail of the sleeping cat. *Yeow!* screeched Big Yellow, who scrambled away as Black Prankster meowed his satisfaction. Kate laughed for the first time in two days.

Her mother laughed too, but then she ruined the fun. "Your teacher called this afternoon. She thinks you may need glasses."

Now Kate found her mother's arm

heavy on her shoulders. She shook it off. "I am *not* going to wear glasses."

"We have an appointment tomorrow with an optometrist."

Kate could not help herself; she stood up and stomped her foot on the wooden porch floor. She wiped a hot tear from her cheek. "I said I am *not* wearing stupid glasses."

"Let's go inside and talk," Kate's mother said. "I have your favorite doughnuts, chocolate with sugar sprinkles."

Kate cried, "Sugar makes me crazy!"

Thursday's Sugar Encounter

·6·

KATE *did* find a way to be absent on Thursday, at least for lunch, recess, and the rest of the afternoon. As she went out the door that morning, her mother gave her a note about an appointment with the eye doctor.

It was cold and gray outside, a mad kind of day. On the way to school, Kate recalled images from last night's dreams.

Grandma Lucy with giant square glasses that were far too big for her delicate face. Uncle Dexter wearing rectangular half glasses that kept sliding down his sweaty red nose. Kate's teenage cousins, Jaren and Jared, wearing small high-tech glasses with thin wire rims. And finally, in a vision that had scared her awake, Kate saw herself behind the biggest, blackest, roundest glasses she could ever imagine. The lenses were so wide you could flip flapjacks on them.

There were no birds or squirrels out on Thursday morning. The sky was so colorless they must have decided to go back to sleep. Kate wanted to go back to bed too, to crawl under the covers and stay perfectly warm all day long. She wasn't paying attention when she kicked a chestnut that sailed straight into the mailman's left shin. "I'm so sorry," she said. "I didn't mean to do that."

"Don't worry, little lady," he replied. "I'm a tough one." The mailman smiled, his eyes blinking behind brushed silver frames.

Kate smiled back and kicked the chestnut further down the street. It landed in a pool of water among some tree roots at the edge of the sidewalk.

"That was quite a shot," said a woman who was watering her mums. Kate had seen her in the neighborhood before, but had never noticed the baby-blue glasses she wore. Were they the same color as her eyes? Kate liked that idea; she would check the woman's eye color the next time she saw her up close. How strange that suddenly the whole world was wearing glasses.

When she got to school, Kate couldn't help noticing how many kids wore glasses. Bobby had round ones. Danny's were rectangles. Megan wore pointy ones with sparkles. Kelsey's glasses were green. Ashley's were gold. Tom's were silver like the laces in his sneakers. Mike's were black just like his hair. Still, Kate could not imagine herself wearing glasses. She didn't *want* to wear glasses.

Just as the first bell rang Sammy Sullivan smacked into Kate's shoulder. "Sorry," he said with a snicker. "Guess you didn't see me."

Hurrying toward the classroom, Kate recognized the sucking sound of sticky rubber soles. Principal Gregory gazed at her through lenses as thick as pond ice. "Have a nice day," he said.

"You too," Kate said. Maybe *he* would have a nice day.

The morning went fast. Kate ducked her head during the Daily Edit again, but she did volunteer to do a math problem on the board. (At least she could still do that.) When the classroom telephone rang she knew her mother was waiting in the school office. "It's time to go to the eye doctor, Kate," Miss Burke announced.

Growing redder by the second, Kate started up the aisle, heading for the row of backpacks at the front of the room. "Good luck," Jenny said, touching her arm.

"See ya later, Spectagator!" Sammy Sullivan made circles with his fingers over his own eyes.

Kate did not want to see the optometrist, and she *definitely* didn't want to wear glasses, but at least she would miss lunch. Kate knew that Jenny would ask the new girl to eat at their table today. Jenny couldn't help being nice to every living thing in the world, and Lauren probably couldn't wait to pull a brush through Sugar's i-n-c-r-e-d-i-b-l-y long hair. As

Kate thought about that hair she came to her old desk, where the real stuff flowed over the back of the seat and halfway to the floor. She tripped over the leg of Sugar's chair, spilling her books across the floor. Kate grabbed her backpack while some of the kids picked up the books. "Don't worry," Rachel whispered. "If you don't like glasses, maybe you can get contacts."

"Thanks." Kate hurried out the door, anxious to be out of sight. She exhaled the huge amount of breath she had been holding in. How silly to be so rattled. How stupid to trip. How completely embarrassing! Then, to make matters worse, Kate had barely gotten out of the classroom when she heard someone behind her. She turned around to find that Sugar Rose had followed her into the hallway.

"You forgot this," Sugar said in her little

bird voice. She held out a bookmark with a map of the world that Miss Burke had given Kate. "It was on the floor under my seat."

Kate had never been this close to Sugar before. She really did have a nose like Barbie's. She had silky hair like Barbie's, and a sugary sweet voice that said "yes, ma'am" all day long. She also had the desk right in front of Miss Burke's neon globe. As a matter of fact, if Miss Sugar Rose Simms had never plunked herself right in the middle of Kate's life, Kate would still be spinning that globe every day. *And* handing out papers. *And* hearing about Sammy Sullivan's detentions. Come to think of it, Kate would still love school. And, besides all that, she would never have had to take the desk at the back of the room. She would not have this stupid appointment today. *And*, she would *not* be getting round or square or triangle glasses with frames in gold or silver—or gel pen pink.

Kate knew that she should swallow them, but the words shot out of her mouth just like Sammy Sullivan's spitballs. "That was *my* seat," she fired. "Why don't you go back to Georgia?"

Kate
and the
Dinoroptor

·7·

KATE'S mother glanced at her in the rearview mirror. "You're pretty quiet back there; everything okay?"

"Uh-huh," Kate mumbled. If she admitted that she had just been as rude as Sammy Sullivan, her mother would insist she apologize to Sugar Rose as soon as possible. Kate didn't want to hear that. And if she described her dreams about the relatives and their strange glasses, her mother would probably laugh. Kate didn't think anything about her situation was funny. Still, if she didn't say something soon her mother might give her the third degree. "I noticed a lot of different kinds of glasses today," she said. "Some of them aren't so bad."

Her mother smiled into the rearview mirror.

A little while later Doctor Schwartz smiled too. "I hear you're having some trouble reading the blackboard?"

"Only since I was moved to a seat that's practically in another state," Kate said, climbing into the examination chair.

Her mother cleared her throat and glared, just like Miss Burke when she was putting Sammy in his place. "I mean, yes, sometimes I have trouble reading the board," Kate said.

The optometrist laughed, his magnified brown eyes twinkling behind thick lenses in copper frames. "Don't worry. When you leave here it won't matter if you are sitting *two* states away from the blackboard."

The doctor began the examination by shining a tiny light into Kate's eyes, one at a time. After that they got down to business with the things she had seen on TV. She identified letters hidden in colorful dot mazes to see if she was color-blind. And, holding a plastic paddle over one eye and then the other, she read a chart with lines of different sized letters. The whole thing was pretty boring, until a big black-and-silver machine with lots of changeable lenses was positioned in front of Kate.

"This is my Phoroptor," Doctor Schwartz explained, obviously thrilled with this part of his job. Kate thought the word *Phoroptor* sounded like the name of a dinosaur. The doctor asked her to lean forward and look into the dinosaur's eyes, and the first lens was clicked into place.

"Wow!" Her left eye saw only black, but everything looked crystal clear to her right eye.

"Pretty amazing, isn't it?" The optometrist's chair rolled closer to the machine. "Now I'll ask, 'Better or worse?' as I change the lenses, and you let me know how it looks to you."

"Got it," Kate said, ready for something to happen.

The Dinoroptor clicked. "Better or worse?"

"Better."

Another click. "Better or worse?"

"Worse."

This went on for a while, and even though Kate grew frustrated when she couldn't tell whether a lens was better or worse, she didn't want it to end. One minute she read an eye chart printed with clear bold letters in deep black ink, and the next minute she saw a chart full of wavy writing in the dullest lead pencil.

Of course, it turned out Kate needed glasses. She was nearsighted, which meant she had trouble seeing things that were far away. That was the reason she could read the blackboard from her old seat, but not from the seat way out in Alaska. It crossed Kate's mind that she could forget the glasses and just move back to the front of the room. But now she was too curious *not* to get glasses. She had already gotten a glimpse of how clear things could look. What would it be like to see that way all the time?

Kate and her mother returned to the main room of the optical store to choose frames. There was a whole wall of them.

"Pick out something you like," her mother said, trying on mini frames in fake tortoise-shell. Her mother didn't wear glasses, and Kate appreciated the privacy she was offering.

She tried on one style after another, staring at herself in long mirrors that hung between the rows of frames. Every shape, every color, some of them two and three times each. Kate wasn't crazy about any of them, but she finally chose small frames with oval lens openings. The plastic was translucent violet, the color of her eyes. Kate turned to face her mother, who had so far kept her opinion to herself. "Perfect," she said.

Since the optical store was in the mall, they went to the food court while the lenses were being made. "We have one hour," Kate's mother said. They walked past several food booths: ice cream, frozen yogurt, French fries, pizza, chicken sand-wiches . . . "Shall we have giant chocolate chip cookies, or those soft maple-frosted pretzels?"

It was just like her mother to mention only the sugary snacks. "I'd like French fries, please," Kate said.

A
New
View

·8·

ON the way back from the optometrist's office, Kate left her new glasses folded in their soft leather case. "Aren't you going to put them on?" Her mother had only seen them for a moment when Dr. Schwartz checked the fit.

"I'll wait until we get home," Kate said. Nobody was going to see her in glasses until she had a chance to get used to them.

But there was something else too. "I know what I want to see first."

Kate put the glasses in her pocket when they stopped to buy *more* athletic socks for Andy. She kept them there when they pulled in at the post office to get stamps. She even left them in her pocket at the grocery store, where the signs that hung high over the aisles were as blurry as the blackboard at school. Kate squinted and pulled the corners of her eyes. Was that *soup* or *soap*? *Pasta* or *pesto*? But she didn't peek through her new lenses.

By the time they got home the sun had broken through the steely gray clouds, and Andy was outside with his baseball gear. He pounced the second his sister stepped out of the car. "Did you get them?"

Kate stopped herself from glaring at him, but just barely. "You'll have to show him sometime," their mother said.

Carefully, Kate pulled the glasses out and put them on. She held her breath. Andy stared at her, biting his lip and bobbing his head like those jiggling little dogs in car windows. "Cool," he said, and ran off to slam as many baseballs as possible. She breathed again and slid the glasses back into the case.

Her mother took the groceries into the house, and Kate stretched out in the grass under her old tree. Above her, hopping from one green-yellow-orange branch to the next, was a small bird. A finch? A sparrow? Kate put on her glasses to see. But then, even though she blinked and blinked, she couldn't believe her eyes!

The maple's swirls of color had turned into individual leaves. Kate saw that each leaf had five pointy tips and delicate veins. She saw that the alligator-skin bark grew smoother further up, and that layers of tiny branches were woven into living lace. Finally, Kate spotted the little bird at the top of the tree. Even from so far away, she could see the salt-and-pepper dashes of the sparrow.

Her eyes were wide open behind the new frames. Kate had never seen so many details before. Everywhere she looked there were small marks or fine lines or tiny dots of colors that she had not seen before. She remembered drawing in the sand at the beach, first with a stone and then with a sharp stick. It was as if everything she saw now had been drawn with the stick; each line, shape, and shadow was perfectly clear. "Mom!" Kate yelled, pushing open the door to the laundry room. "Mom!"

Her mother came running, as if she were expecting blood and broken bones or, at the very least, tears. "What is it?"

"It's everything!" Kate jumped around as if she were in dire need of a bathroom. "Can I borrow your Polaroid camera?"

First she took a picture of the sparrow, which had settled itself on the tire swing as if to say, "Remember me?" Then she photographed the tree and took close-ups of ten one-of-a-kind leaves.

Soon the front porch was layered with Polaroid pictures, instant proof of Kate's new vision. There was no more film, but she didn't stop looking. She cupped her hands around her glasses and slowly, slowly, like a movie camera filming a landscape, turned in a circle on her front lawn. Through those simple lenses, Kate saw that the gray shingles on the house next door were marked with faint green and red stripes. She counted three round knotholes in the door of the mailbox across the street. She noticed tiny specks of black road tar on her father's bumper as his car pulled into the driveway. And then she spotted tiny specks of sweat on her mother's forehead as she came toward her with a new roll of film in her hand.

For once Kate jumped at the chance to watch her brother play baseball. Wearing her glasses and carrying the camera, she walked with her parents to the park. She got good shots of the curiosity on their faces.

The ballpark was old and well used, but the green diamond still glowed in the afternoon's golden light. Kate photographed dugouts full of boys and bleachers full of families. For the first time she noticed that the pitcher on Andy's team had a cowlick at the back of his head, and that the catcher wore glasses. Then, by accident, she saw a brother she never knew. Kate's photographs showed a boy who was focused, fascinated, determined, driven, dedicated—in love. That was it! Andy didn't play baseball because he had nothing better to do; he actually *loved* baseball. He loved catching the ball. He loved seeing it fly through the air. He loved cheering as his teammates rounded the bases. Kate cheered too; her throat was sore by the fifth inning.

As usual, the Slammers won the game. Kate removed her glasses, blew the dust off the lenses, and put them back on where they belonged. She stacked the photographs that were lined up beside her and carefully slipped the camera strap over her shoulder. Then she tucked the camera against her ribs, like Andy carried his glove.

Photography
+
School

·9·

KATE watched car lights creep across the ceiling. She was tired, but too excited to sleep. So much had happened this week. So much had happened in just this one day. Kate never imagined that something good could come from needing glasses, but now she was glad she had to get them. She couldn't wait to take more pictures! Kate was nuts about photography, just like she used to be nuts about school.

Again the room brightened with lights from the street below. Kate sighed. She realized she missed feeling like she was part of Miss Burke's class. But things looked different now. Maybe it wasn't the new girl's fault that Kate hated school. Maybe it was her own choice. And if it had been Kate's decision, then she could just *un*decide. She could simply make up her mind to be nuts about photography *and* nuts about school—even if that made Sammy Sullivan absolutely sick. Especially if it made him sick!

Two more cars passed; two glowing bands lit up the ceiling. Kate watched until both of them had moved all the way across the room and disappeared. "Photography plus school," she mumbled. Photography plus school equals *what*? Mulling over the possibilities in that equation, she finally fell asleep.

Five
Eyes on
Friday

·10·

KATE opened her eyes to find the new glasses staring back at her from the bedside table. Dread spread through her like the flu. Last night she had been so excited that she hadn't thought about what would happen this morning. Today she would have to wear the glasses to school, and everybody would have something to say about them. Would her friends like them? Would people tease her? What if she never got used to them?

She put the glasses on and stood before the mirror over her dresser. She was thinking that the color and shape fit her face, when Sammy Sullivan's voice crept up on her. "Nice look Martin, for a freak!"

Picking up her mother's camera, Kate shook the awful sound from her head. "Ha-ha Sammy," she said. "It's not smart to tease the class photographer." On the way downstairs she called to her mother, "Mom, would it be okay if I took your camera to school?"

"I want you to keep the camera," her mother called back. "You have an eye for photography."

In the kitchen, Kate watched her load several pieces of toast with jam, and set jars of jelly and honey on the table in case someone wanted something sweeter. She kissed her mother's cheek, then snapped a picture of Andy sliding into his chair and knocking his plate onto the floor.

That Friday morning Kate spotted eleven squirrels gathering nuts. The cold clear day was loud with birds gathering to fly south. Their chatter reminded Kate of the cafeteria at lunchtime, and she wondered if Jenny and Lauren had invited Sugar to eat with them. That would be okay, she thought. Today Kate could take candid shots during lunch. She would take pictures of Sammy Sullivan talking with his mouth full.

Miss Burke was putting the Daily Edit on the blackboard when she came in. *Sugar Rose is born in georgia, a state beside the atlantic ocean.* "*Was* born," said Kate. "Capital G on Georgia, capital A on Atlantic, capital O on Ocean."

"Kate," Miss Burke said. "How nice to

see you so early." She did an exaggerated double take. "You look sensational!"

"Thanks." Kate pulled the stack of pictures out of her jacket pocket, and spread them on the teacher's desk. "I have something to show you."

Slowly, slowly, Miss Burke walked back and forth before the photographs. She tilted her head this way and that way, studying the pictures and swinging her sleek hair in every direction. Finally, she looked right through Kate's glasses into her eyes. "These are truly wonderful."

Miss Burke raised her red eyebrows and clapped her hands together. "I have an idea!" She hurried across the room and began to take her *Architecture of Europe* display off the bulletin board, even though it had only been up for one week. By the time Sammy Sullivan raced into the room seventeen seconds after the bell, Kate had covered the entire bulletin board with her pictures. At the top Miss Burke had added

PHOTOGRAPHY
BY
KATE MARTIN

in big blue letters.

Everyone stood around her, looking back and forth between the bulletin board and her new glasses. "Nice tree shots," Christopher said.

Tom whistled as he took in a picture of Andy at home base. "What a slide!"

"I like the ones of the little bird," Rachel said, squinting and leaning closer.

Rachel is probably nearsighted, Kate thought. "My dad put up a feeder," she said. "So it can stay for the winter."

"Aren't Kate's glasses awesome?" Miss Burke said, exaggerating again.

"Yeah," Mike said. "A little nerdy, but not bad."

Kate couldn't think of anything to say, but it didn't matter. Just then Lauren and Jenny pushed their way through the circle of kids and stood in front of her, hands on their hips. "Well," Lauren huffed. "At least now I know what you were so busy with last night. I only called you a hundred times."

Kate laughed. "I'm sorry. I got your messages, but my mom said it was too late to call you back."

Lauren glanced from Kate to the bulletin board and back. "You're forgiven," she said.

"The last I heard, you were just going to get glasses," Jenny said.

"I know," Kate said. "But then everything was so clear, I felt like I was seeing for the first time. Even my own brother looked different."

A gagging sound made everyone look at Sammy Sullivan, who was wearing his now-I'm-going-to-give-it-to-you face. "Don't even think about it," Jenny growled.

Sammy's sly gaze slid around the circle of classmates. Then he took a small step back. "Nice going, Four-eyes," he said.

"Make that *Five*-eyes." Kate glared at Sammy through the eye of the camera. She got a great shot of him with his mouth hanging open.

"Okay, class." Miss Burke clapped her hands exactly as she had when the photo display idea hit her. Now she had another idea. "Let's pose together so Kate can take an official class picture." She began giving directions and moving her students into place, taller ones in the back row, shorter ones in front. On the right end of the first row stood Sugar Rose. Kate had forgotten all about her.

The class stood still long enough for Kate to take four pictures. Then Miss Burke asked the teacher in the next room to take one more so that Kate could be in it too. As the others sat down to do the Daily Edit, Miss Burke turned to Kate. "Since you've already completed that, why don't you go ahead and put the new pictures up on the bulletin board?"

It seemed like such a long time since Kate had walked into the room and pointed out that *georgia* needed a capital G. And it also seemed like such a long time since she had been this happy at school. She thought all the way back to Monday—before Thursday's dreaded appointment with the optometrist, before Wednesday's Daily Edit disaster, before Tuesday's move to Alaska.

But now Kate felt different, stronger. She gave Miss Burke's neon globe a swift spin and watched the whole world go by in flashes of hot pink, zinnia orange, and lizard green. Tacking up the class photos, she noticed that Sugar Rose looked the same in all five shots. She dangled at the end of the first row like a button barely hanging from a thread. Her hands were folded and her shoulders were hunched. Kate saw a small, shy girl in a sweater that was much too big, and she suddenly knew why Miss Burke had given Sugar the desk closest to her own. It had taken all five eyes, but now Kate saw how scary it was to be the new girl in school, how alone and frightened Sugar Rose felt.

Seeing
Sugar

·11·

JENNY and Lauren hadn't gotten the chance to eat lunch with Sugar Rose on Thursday. Instead, after Kate had stormed off to her optometrist appointment, Sugar had gone to the school clinic with an upset stomach. Kate knew that it was really her angry outburst that had made Sugar feel bad, so it was up to her to do something about it.

Every single thing looked different today. It was true that if Miss Sugar Rose Simms hadn't left Georgia and plunked herself in Maplewood School, Kate would still be sitting up front spinning Miss Burke's neon globe. But then nobody would have noticed that she couldn't read the blackboard, and she would not have been hauled off to the eye doctor's or gotten glasses or seen everything she was now able to see. And, worst of all, she would not have borrowed her mother's camera.

Glasses were about clear vision, but photography was about *seeing*. After looking at Sugar Rose in the photographs, Kate wanted to know more about her. As the class walked single file toward the cafeteria, she got out of line and slipped back in behind Sugar. "Hi," she said.

"Hello." Sugar's long hair surrounded her as she turned around. Her face was as expressionless as Barbie's, and her shoulders were just as stiff. Kate could see that Sugar was holding her breath.

"I'm sorry I yelled at you yesterday," Kate said. Now she was the one with the jittery stomach. "I didn't mean what I said."

Sugar wasn't smiling. "Miss Burke shouldn't have given me your seat. You can have it back."

"You keep it. I can see a lot better now," Kate said. "Anyway, there's a hook on the back wall for my camera."

They had entered the cafeteria. The lunch lady seemed to know Sugar Rose already. "Vegetables today?" she asked.

"Yes ma'am." Now she was smiling.

Kate smiled too, and the lunch lady took that as a signal to cover her plate with pale green peas. There was no way she was going to eat them! Jenny and Lauren were waving from their usual table. "Do you want to sit with us?" Kate asked.

Sugar glanced at Kate. "Did you know that your new frames are exactly the same color as your eyes?" She looked back at her plate and moved down the line. "It's my favorite color."

Leading the way to the table, Kate remembered that Sugar's backpack was lavender.

Jenny slid over to make room for Sugar Rose on the bench seat. "Tell us about the beach in Georgia," she said. "I've never seen the ocean."

Sugar was shocked. "Never?"

"Never," Jenny said. "I've been land-locked my whole entire life."

"Yeah, but Jenny is the best lake swim-mer in town," Lauren said. "She looks like a giant prune all summer long."

"Thanks so much," Jenny said, wiping cream cheese from her chin.

Sugar turned to Kate. "Have *you* been to the beach?"

"A few times," Kate said. "In Florida, where my grandparents live." She imagined taking pictures of dolphins as they curved out of the water.

Sugar Rose gazed across the room as if she could see the ocean right there in the cafeteria. "I like to watch the pods of dolphins that swim along the shore."

Kate laughed. "I was just thinking of dolphins! Leaping dolphins."

Sugar laughed too. "Oh, they're incredible leapers!"

Lauren squeezed in next to Sugar and twirled a long lock of caramel hair around her finger. "Do you think I could fix your hair sometime?" she asked.

Just then Sammy Sullivan stuck his nosy self between Lauren and Sugar Rose. "Well, if it isn't the new Peach Pit Barbie and her private hairdresser." He laughed exactly like a cartoon character: "Heh, heh, heh."

Kate stood and snapped a close-up as Sammy Sullivan backed into a boy with a plate full of spaghetti. "Scram, Sam!" ordered Jenny and Lauren in one voice.

When he had walked away, wiping tomato sauce off himself *and* the other boy, Sugar spoke up. "What was that about? Peach Pit Barbie?"

Kate grinned. "We'll tell you all about it if you come over tomorrow." She wrote her telephone number on a paper napkin. "Just call me tonight for directions."

Jenny nudged Sugar with her shoulder. "Bring your shell collection."

"Or your hair clips," Lauren said.

Miss Burke bounced a blue ball across the cafeteria. "Dodge ball," Kate said. "Let's go."

Changing
Colors

·12·

PROPPING the storm door open with one foot, Kate slid her backpack into the laundry room. "Mom, I'm home!" She let the door slam and ran out to the yard.

Kate twisted up her tire swing and climbed on. Spinning, spinning, spinning, she leaned back and looked into a world of orange. It wasn't only leaves that could change overnight. Yesterday she had seen a different Sugar Rose from the small, shy girl she saw now. Kate wondered what she might discover if she took a few more pictures of Sammy Sullivan.

She pushed her glasses higher on her nose, as if she had worn them her whole life. The smile on her face felt permanent. Again, Kate twisted up the tire swing and spun around like Miss Burke's globe. Tomorrow Jenny, Lauren—and maybe Sugar—would swing with her under this tree. By Monday, anything could happen!

The tire circled slower and finally stopped. Kate noticed that the speckled sparrow was eating at the feeder.

Andy stuck his head out the door and motioned for her to come inside. "Mom baked sugar cookies!"

"Sounds good," Kate said.

Author's
Note

WHEN I was a girl there was an old maple tree and a tire swing in our side yard. After school I'd spin and spin, looking up into the leafy umbrella that swirled bright green in the summer and orange in the fall. But it wasn't until I had to get glasses—a dreaded but magical day—that I saw my maple for the magnificent tree it was. "Individual leaves," I said, completely amazed. "Millions of individual leaves!"

And that was it; I was hooked. There was simply nothing better than looking at the world and really seeing it! I took the allowance I had been saving and ordered

Kodak's Hawkeye Instamatic Camera from the back of a cereal box (Cheerios I think), and I've been taking pictures ever since. You can see some of my photographs—even some I took with my old Hawkeye—at www.cynthiabrinson.com.

Have *you* ever looked at the world through the lens of a camera?